A Note to Parents

Welcome to REAL KIDS READERS, a series of phonics-based books for children who are beginning to read. In the classroom, educators use phonics to teach children how to sound out unfamiliar words, providing a firm foundation for reading skills. At home, you can use REAL KIDS READERS to reinforce and build on that foundation, because the books follow the same basic phonic guidelines that children learn in school.

Of course the best way to help your child become a good reader is to make the experience fun—and REAL KIDS READERS do that, too. With their realistic story lines and lively characters, the books engage children's imaginations. With their clean design and sparkling photographs, they provide picture clues that help new readers decipher the text. The combination is sure to entertain young children and make them truly want to read.

REAL KIDS READERS have been developed at three distinct levels to make it easy for children to read at their own pace.

- LEVEL 1 is for children who are just beginning to read.
- LEVEL 2 is for children who can read with help.
- LEVEL 3 is for children who can read on their own.

A controlled vocabulary provides the framework at each level. Repetition, rhyme, and humor help increase word skills. Because children can understand the words and follow the stories, they quickly develop confidence. They go back to each book again and again, increasing their proficiency and sense of accomplishment, until they're ready to move on to the next level. The result is a rich and rewarding experience that will help them develop a lifelong love of reading.

For David
—D. H.

Special thanks to Lands' End, Dodgeville, WI, for providing Josh's clothing, to Penny Lumber, Mattituck, NY, for providing fencing, and to MaryEllen Carlson, The Grandma Boutique, Winona, MN.

Produced by DWAI / Seventeenth Street Productions, Inc.
Reading Specialist: Virginia Grant Clammer

Library of Congress Cataloging-in-Publication Data

Benjamin, Cynthia.
    What's going on? / Cynthia Benjamin ; photographs by Dorothy Handelman.
        p.   cm. — (Real kids readers. Level 2)
    Summary: Josh slowly uncovers the mystery behind the unusual things he has discovered about his new next-door neighbor.
    ISBN 0-7613-2070-9 (lib. bdg.). — ISBN 0-7613-2095-4 (pbk.)
    [1. Clowns—Fiction. 2. Neighbors—Fiction.] I. Handelman, Dorothy, ill. II. Title.
III. Series.
PZ7.B43485Wh   1999
[E]—dc21   98-55129
                                                                                    CIP
                                                                                    AC

pbk: 10 9 8 7 6 5 4 3 2 1
lib: 10 9 8 7 6 5 4 3 2 1

What's Going On?

By Cynthia Benjamin
Photographs by Dorothy Handelman

M

The Millbrook Press
Brookfield, Connecticut

What a day!
Something is going on next door.
Josh sees a truck.
He sees lots of boxes.
"Eat your toast, Josh," says Mom.
But Josh keeps looking.
"Someone is moving in," he says.
"Maybe I will have a new friend."

Josh goes outside.
He sees a woman with a box.
She tips her hat.
"Hello," she says. "I'm Daisy.
I'm moving in next door."
"Hi," says Josh. "I'm Josh."
Then he sees something funny.
What's going on?
Josh wants to know.

8

Josh sees Daisy carry boxes
into her new house.
Mom comes outside. "Josh!" she calls.
"You have to brush your teeth.
You have to make your bed."
"Wait, Mom," says Josh.
"I see something over there."

Josh has found something funny.
Did it fall out of Daisy's box?
What's going on?
Josh wants to know.

Josh takes the comb to Daisy.
"Is this yours?" he asks.
"Yes, it is," says Daisy.
"Thank you, Josh."
She tips her hat,
and Josh sees something funny.
What's going on?
Josh wants to know.

Daisy takes a long, thin balloon
from her pocket.
She blows it up.
She twists it and turns it.
"This is for you," she says.
"Cool!" says Josh. "Thanks!"

Josh goes inside.
He brushes his teeth.
He makes his bed.
Then he goes back outside.
But the truck is gone.
The boxes are gone too.

Josh hears something funny.
He hears music
coming from Daisy's backyard.
He sees balls in the air.
One ball comes over the fence!
What's going on?
Josh wants to know.

Josh picks up the ball.
"Daisy," he calls.
"I have your ball."

"Good!" says Daisy.
"Can you hand it to me?"

That night, Josh thinks about
all the funny things he has seen.
Then he knows what's going on!

The next day,
Josh goes to Daisy's house.
"Hi, Josh," says Daisy.
"What can I do for you?"
Josh grins.
"I want to be a clown," he says.
"Just like you!"

Daisy teaches Josh to be a clown.
She shows him how to do
clown tricks.

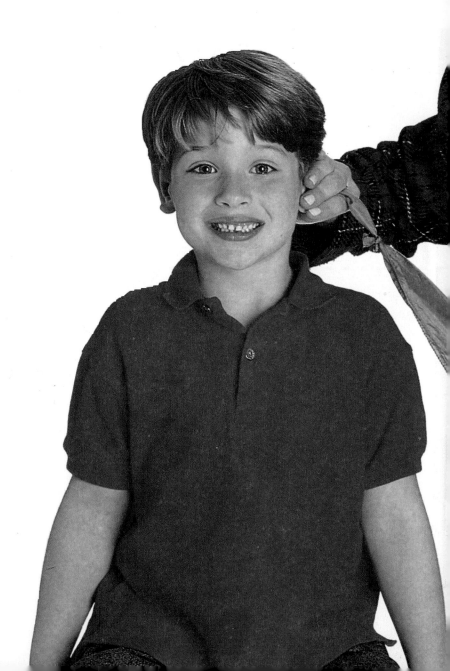

She shows him how to do
clown makeup.

Phonic Guidelines

Use the following guidelines to help your child read the words in *What's Going On?*

Short Vowels

When two consonants surround a vowel, the sound of the vowel is usually short. This means you pronounce *a* as in apple, *e* as in egg, *i* as in igloo, *o* as in octopus, and *u* as in umbrella. Short-vowel words in this story include: *bed, box, but, can, did, has, hat, him, his, lots, Mom, tips.*

Short-Vowel Words with Consonant Blends

When two or more different consonants are side by side, they usually blend to make a combined sound. In this story, short-vowel words with consonant blends include: *brush, grins, Josh, just, long, next, tricks, truck, twists.*

Double Consonants

When two identical consonants appear side by side, one of them is silent. In this story, double consonants appear in the short-vowel word *will* and in the *all*-family words *all, ball, calls, fall.*

R-Controlled Vowels

When a vowel is followed by the letter *r,* its sound is changed by the *r.* In this story, words with *r*-controlled vowels include: *for, hard, her, turns.*

Long Vowel and Silent E

If a word has a vowel and ends with an *e,* usually the vowel is long and the *e* is silent. Long vowels are pronounced the same way as their alphabet names. In this story, words with a long vowel and silent *e* include: *make, takes, time.*

Double Vowels

When two vowels are side by side, usually the first vowel is long and the second vowel is silent. Double-vowel words in this story include: *day, eat, keeps, seen, sees, teeth, toast.*

Diphthongs

Sometimes when two vowels (or a vowel and a consonant) are side by side, they combine to make a diphthong—a sound that is different from long or short vowel sounds. Diphthongs are: *au/aw, ew, oi/oy, ou/ow.* In this story, words with diphthongs include: *clown, found, house, how, new, out.*

Consonant Digraphs

Sometimes when two different consonants are side by side, they make a digraph that represents a single new sound. Consonant digraphs are: *ch, sh, th, wh.* In this story, words with digraphs include: *show, thanks, that, then, there, thin, things, thinks, this, what, with.*

Silent Consonants

Sometimes when two different consonants appear side by side, one of them is silent. In this story, words with silent consonants include: *back, know, night, picks.*

Sight Words

Sight words are those words that a reader must learn to recognize immediately—by sight—instead of by sounding them out. They occur with high frequency in easy texts. Sight words not included in the above categories are: *a, and, be, comes, do, does, from, goes, good, have, he, I, in, is, it, like, of, on, one, over, put, says, she, so, the, to, too, up, want, you, your.*